Dora's Mystery of the Missing Shoes

by Christine Ricci
illustrated by Steve Savitsky

Ready-to-Read

Simon Spotlight/Nick Jr.
New York   London   Toronto   Sydney

Based on the TV series *Dora the Explorer*® as seen on Nick Jr.®

SIMON SPOTLIGHT
An imprint of Simon & Schuster Children's Publishing Division
1230 Avenue of the Americas, New York, New York 10020
Manufactured in the United States of America
6 8 10 9 7 5
Library of Congress Cataloging-in-Publication Data
Ricci, Christine.
Dora's mystery of the missing shoes / by Christine Ricci ; illustrated by Steven Savitsky. — 1st ed.
p. cm. — (Ready-to-read)
"Based on the TV series Dora the Explorer as seen on Nick Jr."
ISBN-13: 978-1-4169-3824-8
ISBN-10: 1-4169-3824-9
0110 LAK
1. Rebuses. I. Savitsky, Steven. II. Title. III. Title: Mystery of the missing shoes.
PZ7.R355Dms 2007
2006029596

Hi! I am 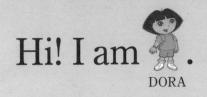 .
DORA

I love playing in the
SANDBOX

at  .
PLAY PARK

The tickles my  !
SAND   TOES

 likes  too!

SWIPER   PLAY PARK

 wants to roller skate here,

SWIPER

but something is missing.

What is missing?

is missing a ！

SWIPER   SKATE

Look! My  is gone!

SNEAKER

We have to find the 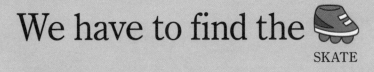 SKATE

and  SNEAKER .

We will be detectives

and solve this mystery!

First, we need to check .
MAP

 says that the and

MAP   SKATE   SNEAKER

are in the .

FIELD

We need to go through the

 and across the .

CAVE   POND

has everything we need

BACKPACK

to be detectives.

Will you find a  ?

MAGNIFYING GLASS

We need the

MAGNIFYING GLASS

to find the tiny

ROCKS

that lead to the .

CAVE

The  is dark.
CAVE

I see a shadow!

What could it be?

It is .
BOOTS

What is  missing?
BOOTS

 is missing his  !
BOOTS   BOOT

We made it to the 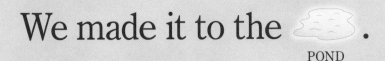 POND .

Look at the ! WAVES

Who is making the ? WAVES

is making the .

BENNY   WAVES

 is swimming.

BENNY

But what is  missing?

BENNY

is missing his !

BENNY   FLIPPER

 is missing his .

BOOTS   BOOT

 is missing his .

SWIPER   SKATE

I am missing my .

SNEAKER

We have to get to the  FIELD

to solve this mystery.

Do you see the FIELD ?

Here at the  I see
FIELD

, , and .

HAY   COWS   WAGONS

Look closely!

Do you see a 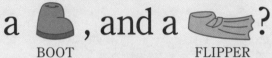, a ,
SKATE   SNEAKER

a , and a ?
BOOT   FLIPPER

Who is wearing

the , 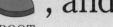, 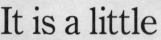, and ?

SKATE   SNEAKER   BOOT   FLIPPER

It is a little !

HORSE

The

The SKATE, SNEAKER, BOOT, and FLIPPER got stuck on the HORSE's feet.

It was a mistake!

We solved the mystery!

This  needs
HORSE

her own shoes.

Do you see **4** 〜〜 ?
FOUR HORSESHOES

The  is happy

HORSE

to have her own  !

HORSESHOES

We are glad to have

our things back!

Thanks for helping!